THE CASE OF THE BURIED BONES

by Lewis B. Montgomery
illustrated by Amy Wummer

The KANE PRESS
New York

Montgomery, Lewis B.
The case of the buried bones / by Lewis B. Montgomery ; illustrated by Amy Wummer.
pages cm. — (The Milo & Jazz mysteries ; #12)
Summary: When a puzzling note and a skeleton are found in place of the town's time capsule, sleuths-in-training Milo and Jazz race with Gordy Fletcher to solve a seventy-five-year-old mystery.
ISBN 978-1-57565-640-3 (library reinforced binding) — ISBN 978-1-57565-641-0 (pbk.) — ISBN 978-1-57565-642-7 (e-book)
[1. Time capsules—Fiction. 2. Practical jokes—Fiction. 3. Mystery and detective stories.]
I. Wummer, Amy, illustrator. II. Title.
PZ7.M7682Cagd 2014
[Fic]—dc23
2013037985

1 3 5 7 9 10 8 6 4 2

First published in the United States of America in 2014 by Kane Press, Inc.
Printed in the United States of America
WOZ0114

Book Design: Edward Miller

Visit us online at **www.kanepress.com**

Like us on Facebook
facebook.com/kanepress

Follow us on Twitter
@KanePress

For Cassidy, the last and best

Titles in *The Milo & Jazz Mysteries* series:

The Case of the Stinky Socks

The Case of the Poisoned Pig

The Case of the *Haunted* Haunted House

The Case of the Amazing Zelda

The Case of the July 4th Jinx

The Case of the Missing Moose

The Case of the Purple Pool

The Case of the Diamonds in the Desk

The Case of the Crooked Campaign

The Case of the Superstar Scam

The Case of the Locked Box

The Case of the Buried Bones

THE CASE OF THE BURIED BONES

Beulah's Burgers

CHAPTER ONE

"Seventy-five years!" Milo said. "That's a long time. I bet they didn't even have computers then."

"Or cell phones," his friend Jazz agreed. She held a five-dollar bill up to the food truck window. "Two corn dogs, please."

The girl took the money and handed her the corn dogs. Jazz pulled one off its stick and passed it to her pet pig, Bitsy. Bitsy swallowed it in one gulp and eyed the second corn dog hopefully.

"Do you think they had corn dogs seventy-five years ago?" Milo asked, popping the last bite of his candied apple into his mouth.

Jazz shrugged. "I don't know."

"Maybe they'll find one in the time capsule," Milo joked. "By now it would probably be a corn dog *fossil*—"

"Milo! Yuck!"

Milo and Jazz were at the park for Westview Day, their town's big yearly celebration. This year it was extra big. A time capsule buried seventy-five years earlier was about to be dug up.

"What's really in the time capsule, anyway?" Milo asked as they walked toward the bandshell. Bitsy followed on her leash, her small eyes fixed on Jazz's corn dog.

Jazz bit off the top. "My dad says people put all kinds of stuff in time capsules. Anything that showed the way they lived back then. Old-fashioned toys, a fountain pen, a comb—"

"A *comb*? We still have combs!"

"Sure, but they didn't know what the future would be like," Jazz pointed out. "Maybe they thought we'd have robots to fix our hair."

Hmm. It was funny to think of *now* as "the future," but that's what it was for people in the old days. And for them, the old days were just . . . *now*!

Milo wondered what life in their town had been like seventy-five years before. What did kids do for fun? What did they learn in school? Did they have—

"Gordy Fletcher!" Jazz said.

Huh?

Milo followed her gaze and groaned. "Oh, no. I thought he'd quit those pranks since . . . you know."

Milo and Jazz were sleuths in training. They solved real mysteries—with help from world-famous private eye Dash Marlowe, who sent them lessons by mail.

Not long ago, they'd solved a case

involving Gordy, the school prankster. Ever since, he had been lying low.

But now, as Milo and Jazz watched, Gordy squatted furtively by his dropped scooter and super-glued a quarter to the sidewalk.

Milo rolled his eyes. "I bet that trick was already around when they buried the time capsule."

Jazz laughed. "I bet it was old then." She finished her corn dog and tossed the stick in the trash. Bitsy gazed after it.

The band played a tune. Then the mayor stepped up to the microphone.

"Welcome, everyone!" she said. "Today

is a special day for our town. We're opening a present—a present from the past."

As the mayor went on, Milo's gaze drifted back to Gordy. He stood holding his scooter with one hand and waving the other, his thumb and pointer finger pressed together in the "okay" sign.

"Gordy seems pretty psyched about the time capsule," Milo said.

Jazz looked over. She shook her head. "I think he super-glued his finger to his thumb."

Milo snorted. Served him right.

The band struck up again. The mayor handed a shovel to the chief of police.

Chief Smalley scooped up a little dirt, and a few people clapped. Then two park

workers came up to do the real digging.

Milo was starting to think about getting another corn dog when, finally, one of the workers said, “I think I hit it!”

The workers cleared away more dirt, then peered into the hole. They looked at each other.

“That’s not the time capsule,” one of them said.

“Nope,” the other worker agreed. “Looks more like . . . *bones*.”

CHAPTER TWO

"BONES?" the mayor screeched.

The microphone blasted her voice through the park. There was a shocked silence, then a growing murmur.

Jazz grabbed Milo's arm. "Come on!"

They squeezed through the crowd, popping out at the front in time to see Chief Smalley grab the mike.

"Now, everyone stay calm," he said. "Please step back from the hole."

The crowd pressed closer.

"BACK!" the police chief boomed.

Everyone jumped away from the hole. The workers jumped too, and dropped their shovels.

"Not you," Chief Smalley told them. "Keep digging. But be careful."

The hole slowly widened. The pile of dirt around it grew.

"It's—it's a human skeleton!" one of the workers said.

They pulled it from the hole.

Milo's mouth fell open. A skeleton? Buried in the park? That wasn't the kind of thing that happened in Westview. That was the kind of thing he read about in stories in *Whodunnit* magazine. Stories about . . . murder!

Suddenly a voice cried, "Herman!"

A very old woman with a walker inched forward. She pointed a shaky finger at the skeleton. "That's Herman!"

Chief Smalley gaped down at her. "Miss Adler, are you saying you can identify these bones?"

"Certainly," the old woman said. "The whole high school knew Herman. What a hullabaloo there was the day he disappeared!"

The mayor looked at the skeleton. "High school? So he was just a boy? How sad!"

Miss Adler leaned over her walker. Her shoulders shook.

"Oh, dear." The mayor fumbled in her purse. "I'm sure I had a tissue. . . ."

The old woman raised her head. Milo saw tears streaking down her face. But she wasn't crying. She was laughing!

The mayor looked bewildered. "What's so funny?"

Miss Adler wheezed helplessly.

Jazz stepped forward. "I don't think Herman was a student. I think he was a skeleton." She pointed. "See the wires?"

Milo saw what she meant. The bones were hung on wires, like a skeleton in a mad scientist's lab.

Catching her breath, Miss Adler explained, "Herman stood in the corner of the science room for years and years. He was a Westview High tradition—until he was stolen."

"Who stole him?" Milo asked.

"They never caught the thief," Miss Adler said. "Of course, we all suspected Gordon Fletcher."

Milo and Jazz stared at each other. Gordon Fletcher? As in . . . *Gordy*?

"That was my great-grandfather!" Gordy yelled, pushing forward.

"Oh? Well, he was quite the cut-up," Miss Adler said. "I'll never forget the time he hid a dead fish in the boys' locker room. What a stench!"

Gordy's eyes lit up. "Really?"

Miss Adler gave him a sharp look. "Oh, yes. Thanks to Gordon Fletcher, our Westview Wildcats were known long after as the Polecats."

"What's a polecat?" Milo whispered.

Jazz whispered back, "A skunk."

"Hey, I remember Old Man Fletcher!" someone said. "When I was a busboy at Beulah's, he came in every day at five.

He used to slip a rubber cockroach in his food to try to weasel out of paying."

Gordy's chest puffed up with pride. His fingers were still stuck together, Milo noticed.

Miss Adler gazed at the skeleton. "Good old Herman. Seventy-five years, and you were right here all along."

"Seventy-five years?" Jazz asked.

Miss Adler nodded. "Herman vanished just before the time capsule went in."

"The time capsule!" the mayor exclaimed. "If the skeleton was buried in its place . . . *where is the time capsule?*"

She flung her hands out, accidentally smacking the skeleton. Its jaw dropped. Something small fell to the ground.

Milo dove to pick it up. It was a

leather pouch—and inside was a folded piece of paper!

"Give me that!" Gordy snatched the pouch from Milo's hand.

The mayor snatched it from Gordy. Then the police chief snatched it from the mayor.

Pulling out the paper and unfolding it, Chief Smalley read aloud:

They found the dead fish
because it was stinking.
But to find the time capsule
will take deeper thinking.
Where is it hidden?
Who'll track it down?
Is there anyone tricky
enough in this town?

G.F.

He looked up. “It’s signed G.F.”

Milo and Jazz exchanged a glance. After Miss Adler’s story, that could only stand for one name: Gordon Fletcher.

“STOLEN!” the mayor shrieked. “The time capsule was STOLEN! Call the FBI! The CIA! The, the—the FDA!”

Chief Smalley's moustache twitched. "That shouldn't be necessary, Mayor. I'm sure we can handle this investigation at the local level."

"We'll find that time capsule!" somebody yelled out. "Even if we have to dig up the whole town!"

In the hubbub that followed, Milo turned to Jazz. "Let's try to find it too! This can be our new case!"

She smiled. "Our new *old* case."

"FORGET IT."

Gordy faced them.

"I'm going to find the missing time capsule, not you," he said, smirking. "Because *I know where it is*."

CHAPTER THREE

Milo and Jazz stared at Gordy.

"Your great-grandpa told you where he hid the time capsule?" Jazz asked. "And you didn't go to the police?"

Gordy threw an uneasy look toward Chief Smalley, who was arguing with the mayor. "He didn't tell me anything. He died before I was even born."

"Then how do you know where it is?" Milo asked.

Gordy grinned. "That's my secret. But

it's somewhere *you* can't go."

"We can go anywhere you can go," Milo protested.

"Not my—" Gordy stopped.

"Your house!" Jazz said. "You think the time capsule is hidden in your house? Did your great-grandpa live there too?"

Gordy's face fell. Before he could reply, a man standing nearby said loudly, "This kid's got the time capsule!"

"What? Who?" someone else asked.

"Him! He says it's at his house!"

"Hey! That's the Fletcher boy!"

Someone grabbed Gordy's sleeve. Wrenching free, he picked up his scooter and pushed off, wobbling as he tried to steer with his stuck fingers. People streamed after him.

Milo and Jazz followed, but slowly. Bitsy outweighed both of them together, and she didn't seem to be in a hurry.

"Can't you make her go any faster?" Milo asked.

"It's hard to rush a pig," Jazz said. "Anyway, we know where Gordy lives."

That was true. Unluckily for Jazz, Gordy lived down the street from her. He was always trying to fool her with some new gag like Fishy Candy or the Gruesome Bloody Finger trick.

"I can't believe Gordy thought we wouldn't guess he meant his house," Milo said. "He's not as clever as he— Hey! A quarter!" Stooping to pick it up, he realized it was the coin Gordy had glued to the sidewalk. Oops.

As he caught up to Jazz, she asked, "Do you think the time capsule is really at Gordy's house?"

"Don't you?"

"They had a picture of it in the paper.

It was a big metal box—big enough to hold a bunch of stuff." She spread her arms to show him. "Wouldn't somebody have come across it by now?"

"Maybe it's in a super-secret hiding place," Milo said. "You know, like one of those bookcases where you pull out a book and the whole wall swings open."

Jazz looked doubtful. "Maybe."

The farther they got from the park, Milo noticed, the slower Bitsy moved. By the time they reached Gordy's house, a small crowd had gathered on his lawn. Gordy's mother stood on the front porch facing them. She looked upset.

". . . fixed it up when we moved in," she was telling the crowd. "We tore out the old plaster walls and put in drywall. There is nothing hidden in this house!"

Milo spotted Gordy's scooter under a tree, but he didn't see Gordy anywhere. He must have slipped inside.

"Maybe it's buried in the yard!" someone called out.

Mrs. Fletcher looked at her colorful flower garden and neatly trimmed lawn. A flash of panic crossed her face.

"NO ONE is digging up this yard." She crossed her arms. "Now, please—GO AWAY!"

Slowly the people began to leave. Milo heard some grumbling about "no sense of history" and "no town spirit."

He turned to Jazz. "So where do we look now? It's been seventy-five years. That time capsule could be *anywhere*."

Jazz looked thoughtful. "I've got a feeling that it's still in Westview."

"Really? Why?"

"Gordon's poem," she explained. "Remember how he ended it: *Is there anyone tricky enough in this town?*"

Milo shrugged. "So?"

Jazz said, "I think Gordon meant he hid the time capsule somewhere in town. We just have to figure out where."

"But how do we do that?" Milo asked. "It was so long ago. It's too late to look for clues at the crime scene or question witnesses or anything."

Jazz frowned. "Well . . . what about Miss Adler? We could question her."

"Good idea!" Milo said. "She might remember— *AAAH!*"

They both sprang back as someone swung down from the tree above them and landed with a thump.

"Gordy Fletcher! You were spying!" Jazz accused.

"Was not! I was hiding from my—um, giving my mom time to chill out. But I heard all your Sherlock talk."

Jazz's hands flew to her hips. "So?"

Gordy grinned. "So . . . let's see who gets to that old lady first!"

With that, he grabbed his scooter and took off.

CHAPTER FOUR

"That rotten sneak!" Milo fumed.

Jazz yanked Bitsy's leash. "Come on! Let's go!"

Milo was sure they'd never catch up, but Bitsy surprised him. As soon as they turned back, the pig put on speed. Soon they were jogging to keep up with her.

"I thought you couldn't rush a pig," Milo said.

"You can't," Jazz said. "But she can rush *herself*."

At the park, Bitsy broke into a sprint.

"I guess she really likes the park, huh?" Milo puffed.

Clinging to the leash, Jazz gasped, "Bitsy! No! *This* way!"

As Bitsy dragged Jazz toward the

food truck, Milo quickly glanced around. Most of the crowd had gone, including Herman and Chief Smalley. The band was packing up. A photographer from the *Westview Weekly* snapped shots of the mayor posing by the empty hole.

Milo caught sight of Gordy standing by a park bench, talking to Miss Adler. As Milo raced toward them, Gordy hopped on his scooter and sped away.

"Miss Adler!" Milo gasped. "I want to talk to you about the time capsule."

She fixed her bright gaze on him. "Yes?"

"I know it was a long time ago," Milo said. "But can you think of anything that might help us figure out where Gordon hid it?"

"Why, that's just what the other young man asked," Miss Adler said, eyes twinkling. "Isn't that odd?"

"What did you tell him?"

She smiled. "I told him he should talk to Charlie Price."

"Who's Charlie Price?" Milo asked.

"Gordon's best friend growing up. The two of them were thick as thieves."

Milo wasn't sure what that meant, but it didn't sound good.

"And he's . . . is he still . . ."

"Alive? Oh, yes," Miss Adler said. "And he hasn't changed much, either, I'm afraid. You'll find him at the Westview Manor Nursing Home."

Milo knew where that was. His class had gone there to sing holiday songs last December. After thanking Miss Adler, he bolted.

Jazz stood in front of the food truck arguing with Bitsy, whose rear end was planted firmly on the pavement. "See that sign? It says CLOSED. No food. The food is gone."

"We have to go to Westview Manor," Milo said.

"I should take Bitsy home first." Jazz tugged on the leash. Bitsy didn't budge.

"But Gordy's already one step ahead of us!" Milo said. "We need to go *now*. After the nursing home, we could stop at Perki Pets for a piggy treat. . . ."

Bitsy's ears shot up. An instant later, she was leading the way out of the park.

As they walked, Milo told Jazz what Miss Adler had said about Charlie Price.

"He must be really old," Jazz said. "Do you think he'll remember much?"

"Miss Adler is old, too, and she seems to remember everything."

"True," Jazz admitted. "You know, there's something about her. . . ."

"What?" Milo asked.

Jazz shook her head. "I don't know. Just . . . *something.*"

When they got to Westview Manor, they saw a man standing near the door. He held the leash of a mournful-looking basset hound. The man and the dog wore matching T-shirts that said PLAYFUL PETS.

Seeing Bitsy, the man brightened. "Oh, good! I was afraid none of the other visiting pets would show up today."

Jazz looked confused. "We're not—"

"This is Elvis," the man said. "Say hi, Elvis!"

Milo offered the dog his hand to sniff. Ears drooping, Elvis looked away.

"Elvis and I come every weekend to cheer up the people in the nursing home.

Don't we, boy?"

Elvis flopped down on the ground and let out a deep sigh.

"We haven't seen you here before," the man went on. "First time?"

Before Jazz could answer, the glass door slid open and a woman with a name tag hustled Gordy out.

"But I *have* to see Grandpa Charlie!" Gordy protested. "He's expecting me!"

"Grandpa Charlie"? Milo was sure Gordy had never heard of Charlie Price before today.

"I'm sorry," the woman told Gordy. "Visitors under twelve must be with an adult." She glanced down at Bitsy, and her eyes widened. "Is that a *pig*?"

Elvis's owner stepped forward. "We're from Playful Pets."

"Oh, yes. Come on in."

"Hey!" Gordy said. "They're not—"

The door slid open. Bitsy plowed after the woman, towing Jazz behind her. Milo followed, and then the man, with Elvis bleakly bringing up the rear.

They were in.

CHAPTER FIVE

Inside, the nursing home smelled like school lunch. Bitsy lifted her snout and sniffed.

Jazz pulled Milo aside. "We shouldn't be in here! We're not with Playful Pets."

"We are now!" he pointed out. "Anyway, Bitsy is a playful pet. At least compared to Elvis."

Jazz couldn't argue with that.

Elvis's owner led them through a set of doors to a long hallway.

"I'll take the rooms on this side," he said, pointing to the right. "You take the other side, and we'll meet at the end."

He knocked on the nearest door and poked his head in.

"Mrs. Russo! Look who's come back! It's Elvis!"

Milo heard a faint groan as the man and dog disappeared into the room.

Jazz said, "We need to find Charlie Price right away."

Leading Bitsy up the hall, they read the names on the doors. De Luca, Johnson, Vega, Lee . . .

"Price!" Milo said.

They peeked inside.

An old man with wispy white hair sat watching TV. On the screen, a cartoon mouse hit a cat over the head with a frying pan. The old man laughed.

"Charlie Price?" Jazz asked.

His eyes didn't leave the TV screen. "What do you want?"

Jazz shot Milo a nervous glance but stepped into the room. "We'd like to ask you a couple of questions, Mr. Price. About Gordon Fletcher."

"Eh?" Charlie Price turned his head. His eyes looked cloudy.

"Gordon Fletcher," Jazz repeated. "Your friend from school?"

"Ha! Fletcher," Charlie Price said. "What's he done now?"

Milo and Jazz traded a look.

"Uh . . . it's about the time capsule," Milo stammered.

A crafty look crossed the man's face. "Time capsule, eh? They won't find it. They'll find something else!"

"Herman the skeleton?" Jazz said.

Mr. Price scowled. "You were always such a know-it-all, Irene."

Irene? Milo thought.

"My name is Jazz. And this is Milo," Jazz said patiently. "We want to know where Gordon Fletcher hid the time capsule he stole."

On the TV, the cartoon cat ran from an angry woman with a broom. Mr. Price laughed again. Then he said, "Fletcher didn't steal the time capsule."

"We know it was Gordon Fletcher!" Milo said. "They found the note!"

"He didn't steal it," Charlie Price repeated stubbornly.

Milo said, "But—"

"Who stole it, then?" Jazz asked. "Was

it you?"

The old man cackled. "I guess this time you don't know it all, do you?"

A nurse pushed a cart up to the door. "Snack time!"

Bitsy's head snapped up.

The nurse rummaged in the cart. "Sliced peaches?" she asked, holding out a foil-covered cup.

Bitsy looked interested.

Mr. Price ignored the nurse.

"Peanut butter on celery?"

Bitsy edged closer.

The nurse put the container back and took out a plastic-wrapped sandwich. "Turkey and sprouts?"

Bitsy strained to the end of her leash.

"Not hungry," Mr. Price said irritably. "Go away."

The nurse shrugged and tossed the sandwich back. As the cart rolled away, Bitsy lunged and broke free.

"Bitsy!" Jazz yelled.

The pig charged out into the hall. Milo and Jazz ran after her. Just as Milo reached the door, he heard a scream and a crash.

In the hall, the cart lay overturned, food spilling out. Bitsy was gobbling down sandwiches, plastic wrap and all. The nurse sat on the floor looking dazed.

Coming out of a room, the man from Playful Pets stopped short. "What . . . ?"

Elvis stopped too. His ears went up. He wagged his tail.

His owner pointed at Bitsy. She had gotten her snout stuck in a foil-covered cup and was butting the downed cart, trying to knock the cup off.

"That's—that's—" The man seemed

at a loss for words. Finally, he burst out, "That's TOO playful!"

Jazz snatched up Bitsy's leash. Together, she and Milo righted the cart and stuffed in as many fallen snacks as they could. Apologizing as they went, they headed quickly for the door.

As it slid shut behind them, Milo heard Elvis barking joyfully.

"At least we cheered *him* up," he said.

Jazz didn't even crack a tiny smile. "That was a disaster."

"Well, you know how Bitsy—"

"Not just that," she said. "All of it. Charlie Price was our best chance to find out where Gordon Fletcher hid the time capsule. And he didn't tell us a thing."

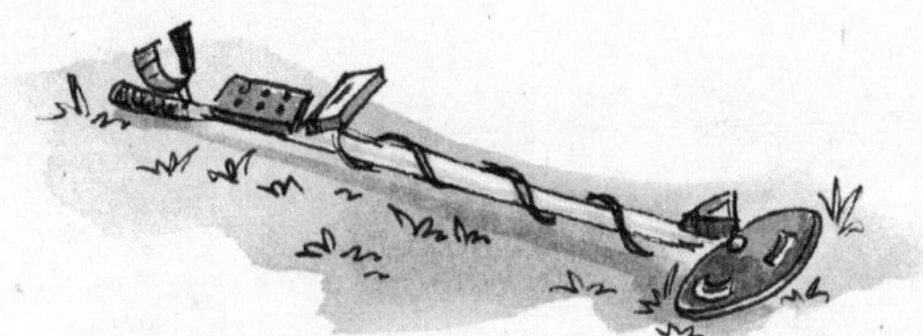

CHAPTER SIX

After the trouble at Westview Manor, Jazz decided to take Bitsy home. "And no stopping for a treat from Perki Pets!" she added sternly.

Bitsy grunted.

When they turned the corner onto Jazz's street, Milo stopped and stared. "What in the world . . . ?"

Gordy's yard crawled with people. Many of them held long-handled black gadgets that resembled weed whackers.

One man was pushing something like a small lawn mower. They all seemed to be wandering around in circles like a dizzy garden crew.

Jazz said, "I think those black things are metal detectors. They're trying to tell if the time capsule is buried in the yard."

As they moved closer, Milo saw that the "lawn mower" was labeled GROUND PENETRATING RADAR.

Gordy's mom stood on the porch dialing a phone. "I'm calling the police!" she announced.

No one seemed to hear her except the man with the radar machine. He stopped pushing and wiped his forehead. "Would you mind calling for a pizza, too? And I could sure use a glass of iced tea. . . ."

Gordy's mom glared at him.

"Or lemonade?" he added hastily. "Anything cold would be just—"

The door slammed.

Gordy sat on a tire swing looking peevish. When he saw Milo and Jazz he slid out and ran up to them.

"Tell me what you found out from Charlie Price," he demanded.

"Why should we?" Milo asked.

Bitsy nosed around in the grass behind Gordy.

"Mr. Price didn't tell us anything," Jazz said.

"You're lying!" Gordy said.

Jazz's eyes widened. "Excuse me?"

Bitsy hunched over and squatted.

Milo said, "Um . . . Jazz . . ."

"You heard me," Gordy said to Jazz.

"You're the one who spied on us and stole our idea," Jazz said angrily.

Gordy smirked. "I can't help it if I'm a

zillion times smarter than you two."

Jazz stepped toward him, fire in her eyes. Gordy stepped back. Milo said, "Watch out for—"

Squish.

"EWWWW!" Hopping on one foot, Gordy peered at the sole of his sneaker and then at Bitsy. "You—you—HOG!" he howled and ran toward the house.

"Oops." Jazz looked at the ground. "I'd clean it up, but it's all mushed into the grass now."

Milo looked too. "It's very . . . shiny."

"That's the plastic wrap," Jazz said.

On the porch, Gordy's mother was pushing him back outside and pointing toward the hose at the side of the house. Milo couldn't hear what she was saying, but she didn't look happy.

"We'd better get out of here," he said.

Jazz watched Gordy for a moment, then glanced down at Bitsy. Her mouth twitched. "I guess you can come along. But no more snacks!"

They walked over to Milo's house. While Milo's little brother, Ethan, played with Bitsy in the yard, they sat on the steps to plan their next move.

"We've got to find that time capsule," Jazz said. "But how?"

Milo rested his chin on his knees. "I've got a feeling Charlie Price knows where it is."

"But he won't tell us," Jazz said. "And we can't go back there anyway, thanks to my *playful pet*."

The mail carrier came up the walk. Taking the mail from her, Milo noticed that an envelope said *DM* in the corner. A new lesson from Dash!

Milo tore it open and read it aloud. Over his shoulder, Jazz followed along.

Make Connections

A string of stolen secrets. A flurry of forgeries. A bunch of break-ins. How does a successful sleuth outthink the outlaws behind these outbreaks of crime?

The key is learning to **make connections**. You might connect two or more similar crimes. You might connect a crime to something you already know. You might even do both, as I did once to solve a rash of robberies on the swanky side of town.

The houses were robbed in broad daylight while the owners were home. The thieves risked being caught red-handed, and yet, every time, they got away scot-free. How? The police were baffled, so they called me in.

I read Dr. Dinero's statement first. She was home alone when her Rottweiler, Bubbles, began to bark in the backyard. Dr. Dinero rushed outside, but Bubbles wouldn't stop. By the time she quieted the dog and went back in, Dr. Dinero's valuables were gone.

The next victim, Mr. Yen, told the same story—except his dog was a yappy terrier named Fred.

By the time I got to Mrs. Moola and her German Shepherd, Maximilian, I knew what connected all the crimes: barking dogs in the backyard. But why would robbers pick houses with noisy watchdogs? It didn't make sense.

I asked myself what I knew about dogs. Dogs are furry. Dogs bark. Dogs have a keen sense of smell. Dogs can hear sounds that are too high-pitched for human ears to hear. . . .

"A-HA!" I said.

"A-HA?" the police asked.

I explained:

"The dog is in the yard. Suddenly it starts barking. The dog barks and barks. The owner rushes out the back door and tries to quiet the dog. Meanwhile, the thieves rush in the front."

"But how do they know when the dog will bark?" the police asked. "And how can they be sure the dog will go on barking until they are done robbing the house?"

I smiled. "Have you ever heard a silent dog whistle?"

They shook their heads.

"Neither have I. Because it's so high-pitched people can't hear it. But dogs can—and if it annoys them enough, they'll bark and bark."

The next day, the police *collared* the dog-whistling thieves. Which reminds me of the time the Vice President's toy poodle was held for ransom . . . but that's another *tail*.

"But we're not trying to solve a rash of crimes," Milo said. "We're just trying to solve one."

Jazz looked thoughtful.

"Stealing the time capsule wasn't Gordon's only prank," she pointed out. "Maybe if we learned more about the other tricks he pulled, we could figure out where he hid the time capsule."

"Miss Adler again?" Milo asked.

Jazz nodded. "Let's go find her right away."

CHAPTER SEVEN

The food truck had left the park, to Bitsy's disappointment and Jazz's relief. The bandstand was empty too.

"Excuse me!"

A plump woman in a tight pink suit teetered toward them on very high heels.

"Can you show me where the skeleton was found?" she asked.

Jazz pointed. The hole had been marked off with bright orange traffic cones and neon yellow police tape. The

workers' shovels lay beside the cones.

"Are you a reporter?" Jazz asked.

"Oh, no," the woman said. "I'm a psychic investigator."

Milo stared. "A *what*?"

She handed him a business card.

BLISS PLOTNICK, PSYCHIC INVESTIGATOR
CRIMES SOLVED – MISSING ITEMS FOUND
NO JOB TOO STRANGE

"I'm here to find the missing time capsule," Bliss Plotnick said.

"By reading someone's mind?" Jazz asked.

"I don't read minds," Bliss Plotnick said. "I sense energy fields. The energy around the hole will tell me where the time capsule has gone."

As the woman hobbled toward the hole, Jazz tugged on Milo's sleeve.

"Come on! Let's go talk to Miss Adler."

"Don't you want to wait and see what the psychic investigator figures out?"

"She's not going to find the time capsule," Jazz said.

"How do you know?" Milo asked.

Jazz looked at him. "Because she couldn't even *find the hole*!"

Oh. Good point.

Miss Adler was still sitting on the same bench, reading a mystery. Seeing Milo and Jazz, she snapped the book shut and set it aside.

"How did it go with Charlie Price?" Miss Adler asked.

"He told us Gordon Fletcher didn't steal the time capsule," Jazz said, making a face.

"You don't believe him, then?"

"The note was signed G.F.!" Jazz said. "Who else could it have been? Besides, Mr. Price seemed a little . . . I told him my name was Jazz, but he called me Irene."

"Irene?" Miss Adler looked surprised. She seemed to be about to say something else, but stopped.

"Miss Adler," Milo said. "Do you remember any more of Gordon's pranks? Besides the stinky fish?"

"And stealing Herman," Jazz put in.

Miss Adler considered for a moment. "Well, there were the chickens . . ."

"Chickens?" Milo asked.

She nodded. "Gordon and Charlie set three chickens loose in the high school with numbers on their backs: One, two, and—"

"Three," Jazz finished.

"No," Miss Adler said. *"Four."*

"Four? But there wasn't any— *Ohhh.*" Jazz laughed. "How long did everybody search for chicken number three?"

Miss Adler smiled. "Quite some time, as I recall."

Milo frowned. The prank was funny, but he didn't see how that would help them find the time capsule. The only connection seemed to be that Gordon enjoyed causing trouble.

Jazz sighed and shook her head. "There's got to be *some* way to solve this case!"

Miss Adler gave them both a long, thoughtful look.

"Now, what did Gordon's dreadful little poem suggest? Deep thinking, was it? I would say that's excellent advice."

With that, she went back to her book.

"We *are* thinking," Jazz grumbled to Milo as they walked away, Bitsy trailing behind them on her leash.

"She's just trying to help," Milo said.

"I'm amazed she can remember so much after all these years."

"That's the problem with this case!" Jazz said. "It's just so long ago."

Milo agreed. "Too bad we can't hop in a time machine and go back to see what happened for ourselves."

Jazz stopped. "That's it!"

He stared at her. "A time machine?"

"Milo, don't be ridiculous. I mean, maybe we can see for ourselves."

"How can we do that?"

"The library keeps old copies of the *Westview Weekly*," Jazz said. "If we can find one from the week the time capsule was buried, I bet there'll be articles—and *photos.*"

Milo's heart jumped. Jazz was right! The old newspaper might hold a clue.

And one good clue could be enough to crack their case.

CHAPTER EIGHT

The Westview Public Library was near the park. As they crossed the street, Gordy sped toward them on his scooter. He had changed his shoes.

"Where are you going?" he yelled.

"None of your business," Milo said, not slowing down.

Gordy rolled along next to them. "You might as well give up, you know. You'll never find that time capsule."

"Why not?" Jazz asked.

Gordy grinned without answering. Then he scootered away.

"He is so annoying!" Jazz grumbled, glancing over her shoulder as they tied Bitsy to the bike rack outside the library.

"Gordy doesn't know anything," Milo said. "He's just trying to rattle us."

Jazz gave Bitsy a pat. "Be good. We'll be out soon."

Inside, the library clerk told them that

the old issues of the *Westview Weekly* were bound into books. Leading them to the shelf, he ran his finger along the row until he came to the right year. He pulled it down and handed it to Jazz.

"Please be careful," the clerk warned. "Those old newspapers are very fragile."

Jazz carried the giant book to a table and set it down. Gingerly, she flipped the cover open and began turning pages while Milo looked on.

"Wait! Stop!" he said.

She paused, scanning the page. "You see something about the time capsule?"

"No, I just wanted to look at that lady's hat." He pointed. "She looks like she's got a tennis racket on her head."

"That's Ginger Rogers," Jazz said. "She

was a big movie star. She sang and danced with a guy called Fred Astaire."

"Did he play head tennis too?"

"*Milo.*" She turned a few more pages, then stopped. "Bingo!"

The headline read TIME CAPSULE BURIED; WILL NOT BE UNEARTHED UNTIL TWENTY-FIRST CENTURY.

A grainy photo showed several men in suits posing with shovels as a crowd looked on. The girls and women all wore skirts or dresses, and the men wore hats.

Milo looked at the photo closely, searching the crowd for teenage boys. Could one of them be Gordon Fletcher or Charlie Price?

Jazz scrutinized the photo too, then shook her head. "I don't see anything."

Time capsule buried
Will not be unearthed
until twenty first centu

She began to turn the page.

"Wait!" Milo said. "Look at that!"

He pointed to a headline at the side: ON THE TRAIL OF A STOLEN SKELETON. STORY, PAGE 7.

Jazz said, "That must be Herman! That could have what we—"

"MILO! JAZZ! COME QUICK!"

They turned. It was Gordy.

He rushed toward them, ignoring the irritated looks from other library patrons.

"Jazz, your pig got loose!" he gasped. "She's freaking out! She knocked a little kid right off his tricycle! He's bleeding! His mom called 9-1-1!"

"WHAT?" Jazz sprang to her feet. "Gordy, if you untied my pig—"

"I didn't do it! She must have chewed

through the leash! She's totally berserk!"

Jazz sprinted for the door, with Milo close behind.

Outside, Milo looked wildly around. Where was the little boy? The tricycle? The raging pig?

"Bitsy!" Jazz ran to the bike rack and

threw her arms around her pet.

The pig let out a startled grunt.

"What . . . ?" Jazz held up Bitsy's leash and looked at Milo. "She's still tied up! Right where I left her!"

It was true. Bitsy had obviously never gotten loose at all.

Milo said, "Gordy and his stupid . . ." He trailed off. Their eyes met.

"Oh, no!" Jazz exclaimed.

They dashed back into the library and ran straight to the table—but they were too late.

The book they had been looking at was gone.

CHAPTER NINE

They searched the library for Gordy, but he wasn't there.

"When we ran out, he must have grabbed the book and sneaked out the back door," Jazz said.

Milo ran up to the circulation desk. "The book of newspapers you gave us—someone took it!" he told the clerk.

"Oh, I don't think so," the clerk said. "Bound newspapers don't circulate."

"He STOLE it!" Milo cried.

"What?"

The library clerk looked alarmed, but there was no time to explain.

Milo and Jazz ran back outside and looked in all directions. No Gordy.

"We'll never catch up to him on his scooter," Milo said. "Even if we leave Bitsy here."

Jazz looked shocked. "Leave Bitsy? After what Gordy did?"

"He didn't actually set her loose," Milo pointed out. "It was just a trick."

"Well, that's true," Jazz admitted. "She was right here where we left her all along."

Wait a minute . . .

"Say that again!" Milo exclaimed.

Jazz gave him a bewildered glance.

"Bitsy was right here all along . . . ?"

Right here all along.

Milo's mind whirled.

A missing pig that hadn't gone anywhere. A puzzling poem that meant exactly what it said. And a confused old man who really wasn't so confused at all.

"THAT'S IT!"

"What's what?" Jazz asked.

"I think I've finally made a connection!"

"Milo, what are you talking about?"

"Come on! I'll explain when we get there!" He dashed off.

Jazz untied Bitsy and ran after him.

She caught up with him at the park. "What are we doing here again?"

"I think Mr. Price told us the truth," Milo said. "Gordon Fletcher *didn't* steal the time capsule."

"He didn't? Then who did?"

Milo was about to answer when a voice boomed, "ARE YOU GOING TO GET OUT OF THAT HOLE OR DO I HAVE TO HAUL YOU IN?"

Chief Smalley stood with his hands

on his hips, staring down into the hole where Herman had been found.

Milo and Jazz ran up to the edge of the area marked off by traffic cones and tape. Peering into the hole, all Milo saw at first was a large, bulging object covered in pink cloth. Then he realized it was Bliss Plotnick's rear end. She was on her hands and knees inside the hole.

The psychic investigator looked up at Chief Smalley. "Please stop shouting. You'll disturb the energy."

His face turned as pink as her suit. "The *energy*?"

Bliss Plotnick sat back on her heels. "I'm trying to sense the energy left behind by the missing time capsule."

"Well, you'll have to sense it on the other side of *this*," Chief Smalley said, jabbing a finger at the police tape.

"Oh, no," Bliss Plotnick told him. "That won't work. I need to be able to touch and smell." She got down on her hands and knees again and took a long, loud sniff.

"You can smell the time capsule?" Milo asked.

"It's very faint," Bliss Plotnick said. "It's been gone a long, long time."

Milo said, "Actually, I don't think it's gone at all."

Everyone looked at him.

"It's like Gordy's trick with Bitsy!" he told Jazz. "He told us she had gotten loose, so we believed him. Just like we all believed the time capsule was gone."

"What do you mean?" Chief Smalley said. "Of course the time capsule is gone. We dug for it but found the skeleton instead."

"You found it *first,*" Milo corrected, "and didn't bother digging any further, thanks to Gordon's sneaky poem."

Jazz's face lit up. "Gordon never said the time capsule was gone, did he? He only said that finding it would take—"

"*Deeper thinking,*" Milo finished, looking into the hole. "In other words, figuring out that the time capsule was buried *deeper* in the ground."

"So Mr. Price was right!" Jazz said. "Gordon *didn't* steal the time capsule. He didn't even dig that far down."

Milo nodded. "The time capsule had just been buried. It was the perfect place to hide the stolen skeleton. All he had to do was shovel out some of the loose dirt and put Herman in on top—"

"Along with a note to make us *think* he'd pulled a switch!" Jazz finished. "When really, the time capsule was right where it had been all along."

Bliss Plotnick stood up and brushed herself off. She held out a hand to Chief Smalley. "Can you help me out?"

Chief Smalley's moustache twitched. "No . . . but you can help *me* out."

He handed her one of the shovels.

Taking the other one, he jumped into the hole with her and they began to dig.

When they heard the clunk of metal, the chief and Bliss climbed out and let Milo and Jazz hop down into the hole.

Crouching, Milo brushed the loose dirt away. A patch of silver gleamed.

"I'm sensing that's the time capsule," Jazz joked.

Milo grinned. "Yeah. I sense it too."

DAY!
Beulah's Burgers

CHAPTER TEN

"Three corn dogs, please," Milo said, holding out his money to the girl inside the food truck window.

"*Three?*" Jazz asked.

"Sure. I'm getting one for Bitsy, too. It's the least I can do, after she helped us solve our case."

They were at the park, where the grand opening of the time capsule had just taken place. Bitsy gulped down her corn dog, then followed Milo and Jazz over to the tables where the contents of the time capsule stood on display under Chief Smalley's watchful gaze.

Jazz stopped to look at a black-and-white photo. "Here's a picture of the high school's graduating class."

Milo pointed to a boy in the back row.

"That must be Gordon Fletcher."

Jazz leaned in closer. "Are you sure? He doesn't look anything like Gordy."

"See the girl next to him?"

Jazz groaned. "Bunny ears."

Milo nodded. The boy was holding up two fingers behind the girl's head. Definitely Gordon.

"Milo!" Jazz grabbed his arm. "Look! The *Westview Weekly*!"

It was the same issue they'd seen at the library, with the front-page article about the time capsule and the mention of the stolen skeleton.

"We never did get to read that article," Jazz said.

"Yeah, thanks to Gordy," Milo said.

Carefully he turned to page seven. Below a headline reading STOLEN SKELETON STUMPS STUDENT SLEUTH was a photo of a bright-eyed teenage girl.

Milo read aloud: "No wrongdoer has ever managed to outwit Westview's own clever girl detective, Irene Adler. But the recent theft of—"

"Irene *Adler*!" Jazz exclaimed.

"Yes, dear?"

Miss Adler stood behind them, leaning on her walker and smiling.

"Westview's girl detective, huh?" Jazz nudged Milo. "I told you there was something about her! No wonder Charlie Price called me Irene."

"You figured it out first, didn't you, Miss Adler?" Milo said. "You knew what Gordon's note meant way before we did."

The old woman patted his arm. "You're the detectives now. It was your case to solve. And you solved it!"

"It wasn't easy," Milo said. "Especially with Gordy getting in our way."

"I saw that young man yesterday. He was at Westview Manor playing cards with Charlie Price," Miss Adler said. She added, "They were both trying to cheat."

Milo laughed. Figured.

Jazz said, "Gordy has to visit the nursing home as his community service. For stealing from the library."

"I'm glad they got the book back," Milo said.

"Yes, indeed," Miss Adler agreed. "We wouldn't want any more of our local history to disappear!"

The microphone squawked, and everyone looked up at the bandstand, where the mayor stood.

WestView Weekly
W

"I have a special announcement," she said. "The town council has voted to bury a new time capsule, to be opened seventy-five years from today. And the first item to be placed in it will be this issue of the *Westview Weekly*."

Holding up a newspaper, she read the headline aloud: "YOUNG SLEUTHS DIG UP SOLUTION TO 'MISSING' TIME CAPSULE. Thank you, Milo and Jazz!"

The crowd cheered, and the mayor stepped away.

"Can you believe it?" Jazz said. "Seventy-five years from now, people in Westview will be reading about *us*!"

"What do you think will happen in the next seventy-five years?" Milo asked. "Do you think we'll stay friends?"

"Of course!" Jazz said. "And partners. We'll be world-famous private eyes, just like Dash Marlowe. And then when we're really old, we can retire and come back to Westview to see the time capsule get dug up."

"With Bitsy's great-great-great-great-grandpigs," Milo said.

Jazz laughed. "And we can visit Herman at the high school."

She pointed at the old skeleton. Dusted off and polished, Herman hung from a gleaming new frame, wearing a giant, toothy grin.

Milo couldn't help grinning back.

SUPER SLEUTHING STRATEGIES

A few days after Milo and Jazz wrote to Dash Marlowe, a letter arrived in the mail. . . .

Greetings, Milo and Jazz,

Congratulations! Mysteries from the past are always tricky, and this one was a doozie, what with a skeleton, a time capsule, and a deceased prankster. (Solving it sure took some digging!) You two have amazing detecting talent. I predict you'll have long, long careers ahead of you. Today Westview, tomorrow, the world!

Happy Sleuthing!

—Dash Marlowe

Warm Up!

Here are some brain stretchers to warm you up! The answers are at the end of this letter.

1. Why did the boy bury his flashlight?
2. How can a pants pocket be empty and still have something in it?
3. Take away my first letter and I still sound the same. Take away my last letter and I still sound the same. I am a five-letter word. What am I? (Hint: The answer is a word used in one of the other questions. . . .)
4. You are running in a marathon and you overtake the person in second place. What place are you in now?

The Muddled Time Capsule: An Observation Puzzle

The town of Muddle buried a time capsule to be opened in 100 years. "It will be full of items that will show everyday life right now!" declared the mayor. But wait a minute. Five items in that capsule are way too old-fashioned to be from life "now." Observe closely, and see if you can pick them out!

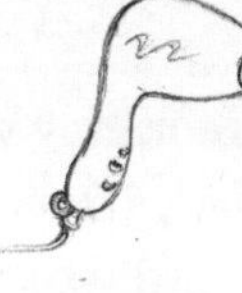

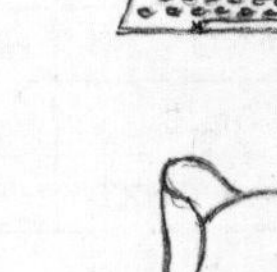

Answers: 1) Old-fashioned phone: Back in 1920, this baby would have been just the thing. 2) Knight's helmet: Not typical of headgear in modern Muddle. 3) Old typewriter: I'll bet you know what came along and replaced this item. 4) Three-corner hat and 5) feather pen / ink stand: The same guys who wore the hat would have used the pen—about 250 years ago!

That's It! A Logic Puzzle

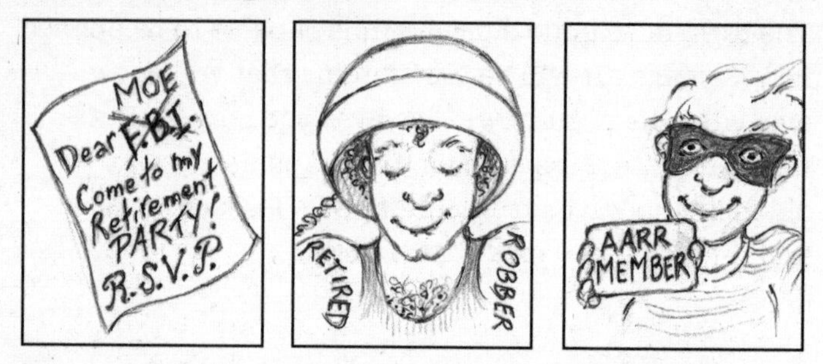

Three ex-robbers were recalling why they decided to give up robbery and retire. What made each guy decide he was losing his edge? And what did he do next?

Look at the clues and fill in the answer box where you can. Then read the clues again to find the answer.

Answer Box *(see answers on next page)*

	Rocky	Louie	Sal
Why he quit			
What was next			

1. Rocky forgot to wear his glasses and ended up stealing a red jellybean that he thought was a ruby.
2. Louie almost got caught on his last heist because he didn't hear the burglar alarm.
3. Sal was not the robber who had to be talked out of inviting the FBI to his big retirement party.
4. One robber had a makeover.
5. Louie joined the AARR (Association of Retired Robbers).
6. Another guy went to a bank to rob it but forgot why he came and opened an account instead.

Pay Up! A Mini-Mystery

Check out this case—and draw your own conclusion!

A client, Roderick Doss, came to me looking sick with worry. He told me why. "A man I knew long ago, Hiram Huber, showed up out of the blue insisting that I owe him $20,000! I don't remember any such thing, but Huber said he loaned me the money years ago when I was in debt and he was flush. He told me it was around the holidays so I was feeling especially strapped. And then"—Doss turned pale—"Huber said he had proof! He showed me a check, drawn on the Honest Bank and Trust on November 31, 2003, for $20,000. The check was made out to me, Roderick Doss, and was marked PAID!"

At that, Doss pulled the check out of his pocket and handed it to me. I patted his shoulder and said, "Relax. You have nothing to worry about. The check is a fake." How did I know?

Answer: I knew Huber was scamming Doss because there is no November 31. And I was ready to bet that no "Honest Bank"—or even a dishonest one—would accept a $20,000 check with a date that doesn't exist!

Answer to Logic Puzzle: When Rocky realized he'd stolen a jellybean instead of a ruby he threw himself a great retirement party, even if he did get talked out of inviting the FBI. After Sal mistakenly opened a savings account instead of robbing a bank, he had a makeover and got a stunning Retired Robber tattoo. Louie almost got caught on a heist when he didn't hear the alarm, so he joined AARR and got a great deal on a hearing aid.

QUACK! A Making Connections Puzzle

Farmer Zeke's prize duck, Mabel, was ducknapped! Zeke had several suspects in mind—and plenty to say about them! Who seems like the best bet? Think, make connections to experiences you've had, things you've noticed about people, facts you know. . . . Then compare your connection-making with mine!

1. Dina Duckmeir, who hated ducks.
2. Wilma Webb, who had had six pet ducks, and always said they were the "six best ducks in the world." ("Jealous!" Zeke said.)
3. Al Dix, watchman at a car lot, kept complimenting Mabel. ("Bet he wanted Mabel for a guard duck!")
4. Petal Smith, an eight-year-old who asked for a pet duck for her birthday but didn't get one. ("Brat!")
5. Seth Zuker, a filmmaker, wanted to sign Mabel for his new flick, *The Demon Duck*. He said, "Mabel has the most terrifying quack I've ever heard!" But Zeke said no. "Allow Mabel to play an evil duck? Never!"

My thinking: 1. Someone like Dina who hates ducks would want nothing to do with them. 2. Wilma was happy with the six ducks she had. Why would she want another one? 3. A guard duck? Ridiculous. 4. Petal? Hmm. 5. Zuker wouldn't ducknap Mabel for his film because he'd get caught! The minute Zeke found out the film was getting made, he'd know what happened to Mabel.

Answer: Yep, Petal did it. She unhooked Mabel's cage and walked off with her. I found a very contented-looking Mabel in Petal's toy closet, wearing a big blue bow and eating cookie crumbs. (The quacking was a giveaway.)

Answers to Brain Stretchers:

1. The batteries had died.
2. It can have a hole in it.
3. EMPTY
4. Second

Praise for . . .

"**The Milo & Jazz Mysteries** is a series that parents can enjoy reading with their children, together finding the clues and deducing 'whodunit'. The end of book puzzles are a real treat and will likely challenge most readers, regardless of age level."—*Mysterious Reviews, Hidden Staircase Mysteries*

"Certain to be a popular series, **The Milo & Jazz Mysteries** are highly recommended additions to school and community library collections for young readers."—*Midwest Book Review*

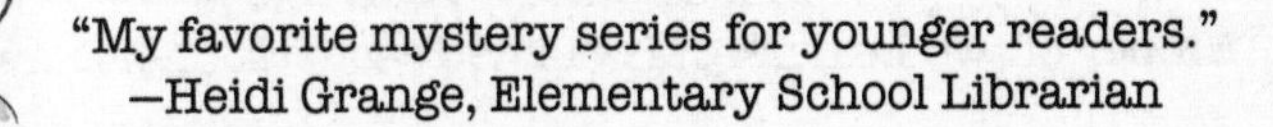

"My favorite mystery series for younger readers."
—Heidi Grange, Elementary School Librarian

★ ***Booklist* STARRED REVIEW** and
Book Links' Best New Books for the Classroom
for *The Case of the Stinky Socks*:
"Gets it just right."

Agatha Award nominee for Best Children's Mystery
The Case of the Poisoned Pig

Moonbeam Children's Book Awards
The Case of the July 4th Jinx: Silver Medalist
The Case of the Superstar Scam: Bronze Medalist

Visit **www.kanepress.com** to view
all titles in The Milo & Jazz Mysteries.

Check out these other series from Kane Press!

HOLIDAYS & HEROES

(Grades 1 & Up • Ages 6 & Up)

"The Holidays & Heroes series commemorates the influential figures behind important American celebrations. Written with emerging readers in mind, this volume emphasizes the importance of lofty ambitions and fortitude in the face of adversity.... A mix of full-color illustrations and period photographs facilitates comprehension and encourages discussion."—*Booklist* (for *Let's Celebrate Martin Luther King Jr. Day*)

(Grades PreK–3 • Ages 3–8)

Winner of two *Learning* Magazine Teachers' Choice Awards

"A great product for any class learning about letters!"
—*Teachers' Choice Award reviewer comment*

LET'S READ TOGETHER®

(Grades PreK–3 • Ages 4–8)

"Storylines are silly and inventive, and recall Dr. Seuss's *Cat in the Hat* for the building of rhythm and rhyming words. This helpful series for emerging readers will engage their attention and be fun at the same time."
—*School Library Journal*

(Grades K–3 • Ages 5–9)
Winner of a *Learning* Magazine Teachers' Choice Award

"These cheerfully illustrated titles offer primary-grade children practice in math as well as reading."—*Booklist*

(Grades PreK & Up • Ages 4 & Up)
"A cheerful addition to the growing list of math-related picture books. The artwork is lively and expressive...and [the math concept is] well supported by the story and illustrations."—*Booklist* (for *The Mousier the Merrier!*)

(Grades K–3 • Ages 5–9)
"The Science Solves It! series is a wonderful tool for the elementary teacher who wants to integrate reading and science."—*National Science Teachers Association*

(Grades K–3 • Ages 5–9)
"This series is very strongly recommended..."
—*Midwest Book Review*

ABOUT THE AUTHOR

Lewis B. Montgomery is the pen name of a writer whose favorite authors include CSL, EBW, and LMM. Those initials are a clue—but there's another clue, too. Can you figure out their names?

Besides writing the Milo & Jazz mysteries, LBM enjoys eating spicy Thai noodles and blueberry ice cream, riding a bike, and reading. Not all at the same time, of course. At least, not anymore. But that's another story. . . .

ABOUT THE ILLUSTRATOR

Amy Wummer has illustrated more than 50 children's books. She uses pencils, watercolors, and ink—but not the invisible kind.

Amy and her husband, who is also an artist, live in Pennsylvania . . . in a mysterious old house which has a secret hidden room in the basement!